Anthony Ant's MYSTERY Midnight Feast

Lorna and Graham Philpot

Dolphin

Crazy maze

Giant word search

Spot the difference

Bigfoot's boot

Web maze

Where's Weevil witch?

Hidden shapes

Which root?

Unpack the rucksack

Plot the route

Flower hopping

Rug race

Anthony Ant has had a mystery message on his extra-sensory antennae.

THERE'S A MIDNIGHT FEAST AT BIGFOOT'S HOUSE PLEASE COME AND BRING YOUR FRIENDS

Anthony Ant is very excited. He calls all his friends and tells them to meet him along the way.

Anthony Ant packs his rucksack, and in it he puts a tent, a sleeping bag, a torch, a compass, a map, a magnifying glass, a whistle, a pocket knife, a ball of string, a pencil, a notebook, a pair of binoculars, a bottle of aphid milk, a carton of Fungal Jungle juice, a chocolate chip cookie, a sugar lump, a tube of toothpaste, a toothbrush and some spare pants and socks.

Take a good look at these objects and remember what they are so you can play the UNPACK THE RUCKSACK game later.

Now help Anthony Ant
PLOT THE ROUTE
on his map.

1. Plumtree Tower........B2
2. Fungal Jungle........D2
3. Rotten Wood.........G3
4. the Great Bean Forest..C9
5. Spider's Web Bridge...K8
6. Pebble Rock........M10
7. Flowerpot House......N8
8. Crazy Paved Path.....Q6
9. Yellowstone Wall.....S1
10. Pinetree Table.....U12

SCALE: 1mm to 30 millimetres

0   0.9M   1.8 Metres

0   900mm   1800mm

Bee Hive

Compost Hill

A   B   C   D   E   F   G

1   Aphid Farm

2   Plumtree Tower   FUNGAL JUNGLE

Wee Witi Cav

3   Mushroom Cottage   ROTTEN WOOD   Fungus Farm

4   N   Woodlouse House

5

6   W   E   The Grasslands of the Outback Lawn

7   S

VEGETABLE

8   GARDEN   The Great Bean Forest

9   Termite Tower

Old Digger Ant's Goldmine

10   Jack's Town

SANDPIT PLAIN

11   Ant Tea House

12   Pyramid Rock Tomb of Tutantcocoon   Pine Tree Towers   PINETREE

A   B   C   D   E   F   G   PARK

4

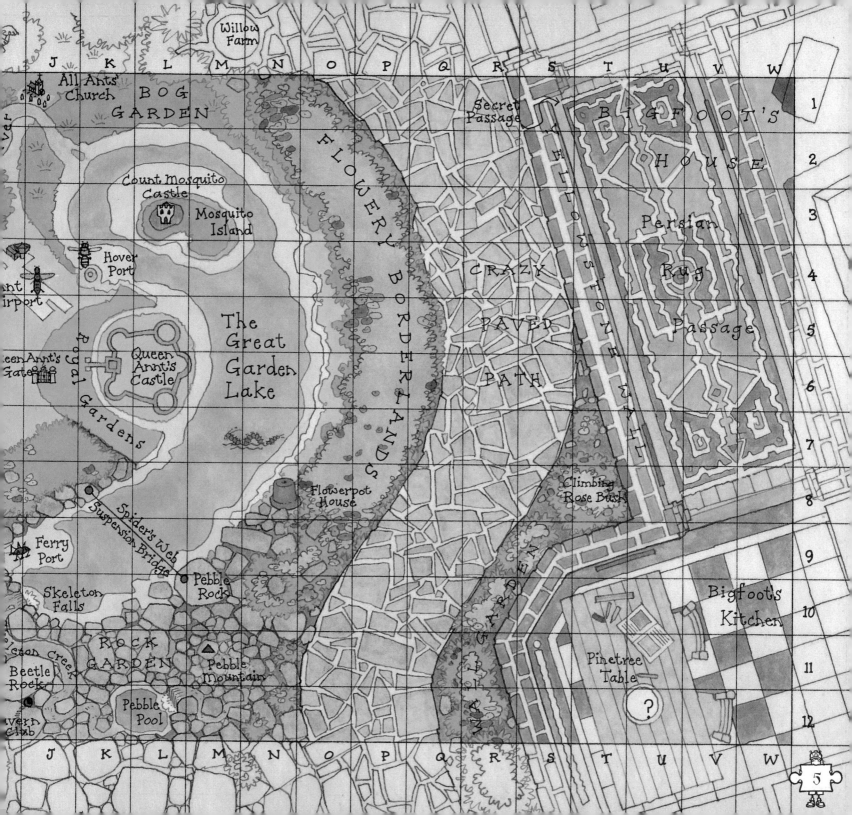

Willow Farm

J K L M N O P Q R S T U V W

All Ants' Church

BOG GARDEN

Secret Passage

BIGFOOT'S

HOUSE

1

2

Count Mosquito Castle

Mosquito Island

FLOWERY BORDERLANDS

Persian

3

Hover Port

CRAZY

Rug

4

...nt ...irport

PAVED

Passage

5

...een Annt's Gate

Queen Annt's Castle

The Great Garden Lake

PATH

6

Royal Gardens

7

Climbing Rose Bush

8

Spider's Web Suspension Bridge

Flowerpot House

9

Ferry Port

Skeleton Falls

Pebble Rock

Bigfoot's Kitchen

10

...lston creek

ROCK GARDEN

Pebble Mountain

GARDEN PLAZA

Pinetree Table

11

Beetle Rock

Pebble Pool

?

12

...vern Club

J K L M N O P Q R S T U V W

5

Prepared and ready for anything, Anthony Ant sets off with his trusty pet aphid, Aphido, to meet Kevin Ant, Alexi Ant and Billy Bedbug, who all live in Plumtree Tower.

Anthony Ant needs something from his rucksack right away. What is it? Don't look at page 3!

APHID ALLEY

6

Their first task is to get out from underground into the Great Outdoors.

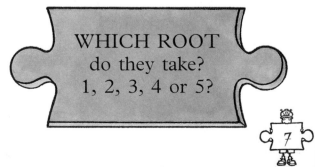

WHICH ROOT
do they take?
1, 2, 3, 4 or 5?

7

Once they are in the Great Outdoors, they must go to Fungus Farm, on the edge of Rotten Wood, to meet Ruby Red Ant and Lucy Woodlouse.

To Fungus Farm

Rotten Wood is surrounded by the Fungal Jungle. The Fungal Jungle is an eerie place. Things move, faces appear and colours change . . .

SPOT THE DIFFERENCE
There are 16 things that are different in these two pictures.

Look and see what Anthony Ant has taken out of his rucksack now.

Anthony Ant and his friends have arrived in the Great Bean Forest to meet Bobby Ant and Terry Termite. They're a bit early, so they stop for a picnic.

While they wait they play a game. They all look for hidden shapes in the forest.

Termite Tower

Can you find the HIDDEN SHAPES?
A bird, a mouse, a rabbit,
a hedgehog, a lizard,
a butterfly, a moth, a ladybird,
a slug, 3 frogs and 5 snails.

11

To get to Pebble Rock where
Jeremy Beetle and Rocky Ant are waiting,
Anthony Ant and his friends must cross the
Great Garden Lake by the Spider's Web
Suspension Bridge.

It's a bit risky. It would not be wise to wake the
sleeping spiders!

Help Anthony Ant and his
friends find their way through
the WEB MAZE.
Do not cross the spiders!

PONDSKATER
FERRY-
Mosquito
ISLAND

Pebble
Rock

Bungy Jumping £2·50

Pebble Rock

13

After picking up Kitty Caterpillar and Georgie Ant from Flowerpot House they must cross the Flowery Borderlands to Bigfoot's house. They decide to play one of their favourite games, FLOWER HOPPING.

The game is to hop from flower to flower in colour order - red, orange, yellow, blue, purple, pink, red. See if you can follow the route from red flower A to red flower B.

Flowerpot House

A

14

What has Anthony Ant taken out of his rucksack now? Don't look at page 3!

To help you, there's a bumblebee on every red flower along the route.

Now they must cross Crazy Paved Path and find the secret passage through Yellowstone Wall into Bigfoot's house. They must keep to the cracks or Bigfoot will get them!

There are 16 animal shapes on the sole of BIGFOOT'S BOOT. What are they?

←Secret Passage

BIGFOOT'S HOUSE

Can you find your way through the CRAZY MAZE, avoiding all the slimy slugs and snails who block the trails?

READY · STEADY · GO

Anthony Ant and his friends are inside Bigfoot's house at last! They've found two wind-up toy cars to help them on their long journey down Persian Rug Passage to Bigfoot's kitchen.

See who wins the RUG RACE! There are two separate ways across the rug, and the cars can only drive on the yellow tracks. Time how long each route takes.

KITCHEN

Anthony Ant can smell the feast, but it's way up high on the Pinetree table at the top of a gigantic carved pinetree leg. Rocky the climbing ant leads the way.

19

GIANT
WORDSEARCH PUZZLE
The words can be found across, down or diagonally

A	S	P	I	D	O	R	O	C	K	Y	A	N	T	H	O	N	R	Y
A	N	T	H	B	E	E	U	G	I	N	L	O	U	S	N	A	L	L
C	A	T	C	U	I	A	U	B	T	B	U	G	S	A	L	E	X	J
B	I	N	I	A	S	L	U	C	Y	W	O	O	D	L	O	U	S	E
S	L	O	T	P	P	I	L	L	E	R	A	B	I	E	U	S	G	R
W	U	L	T	H	E	X	I	Y	W	E	E	P	B	X	G	A	T	E
E	C	K	Y	I	O	E	K	Y	B	D	R	D	H	I	D	N	A	M
E	K	J	G	D	A	N	T	I	W	E	E	W	A	A	A	T	N	Y
V	Y	L	E	O	U	W	Y	A	T	N	D	E	I	N	A	N	T	B
I	G	E	O	R	G	I	E	A	N	T	J	B	I	T	T	Y	T	E
L	A	X	G	R	E	D	C	E	N	W	E	V	U	L	D	M	I	E
W	A	I	I	D	O	Y	R	O	V	T	E	C	I	G	E	O	R	T
I	B	P	E	I	T	C	M	G	C	K	R	R	A	N	T	H	I	L
T	A	N	H	T	E	R	R	Y	T	E	R	M	I	T	E	O	A	E
C	S	P	I	D	E	R	C	N	J	E	B	O	B	B	Y	A	N	T
H	A	K	H	O	L	U	A	H	T	O	N	Y	A	N	T	P	T	Y

The hidden words are: ANTHONY ANT, APHIDO, KEVIN ANT, ALEXI ANT, BILLY BEDBUG, RUBY RED ANT, LUCY WOODLOUSE, BOBBY ANT, TERRY TERMITE, ROCKY ANT, JEREMY BEETLE, GEORGIE ANT, KITTY CATERPILLAR and WEEVIL WITCH. Also SPIDER, SLUG and SNAIL.

20

It's nearly midnight and they are very close, but there is one last distraction. Bigfoot has left a puzzle book open on the pinetree table.

Help them find their names in this GIANT WORDSEARCH!

Anthony Ant takes out one more thing from his rucksack. What is it?

Anthony Ant and his friends all find their names. Then they have one final climb up a great china column. What kind of feast will they find up there?

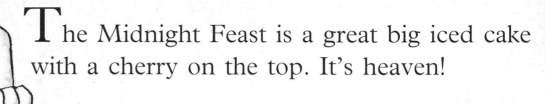

The Midnight Feast is a great big iced cake with a cherry on the top. It's heaven!

And who do you think sent the mystery message? It was Anthony Ant's old friend Quincy Spider, who lives in a corner of Bigfoot's kitchen ceiling!

WHERE'S
WEEVIL WITCH?
Did you see her following
Anthony Ant along the way?

ANSWERS:

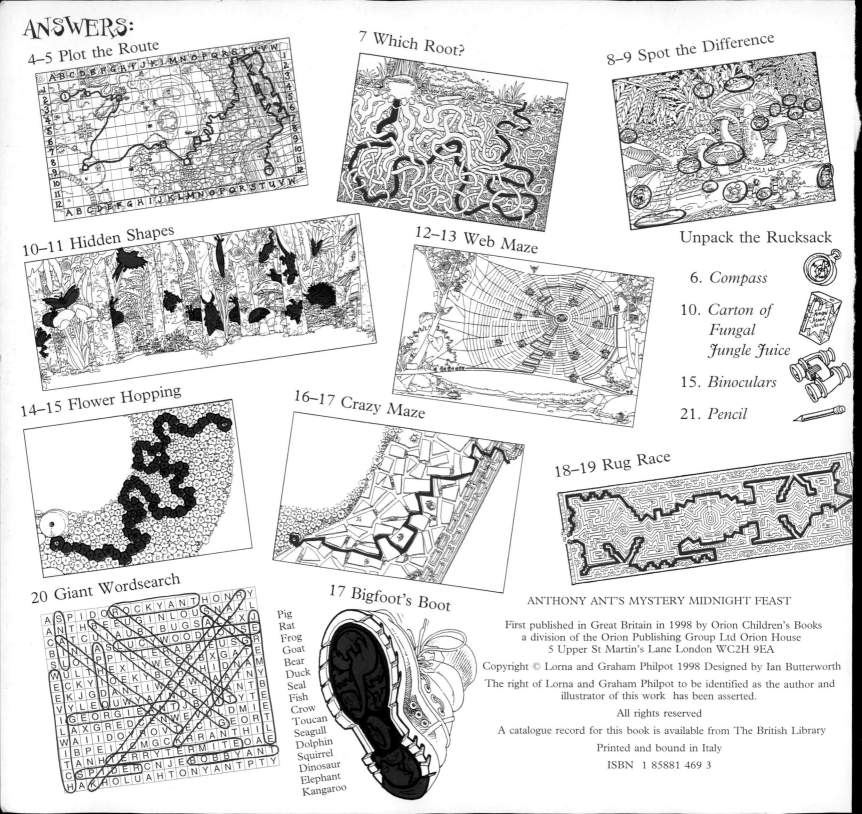

4–5 Plot the Route

7 Which Root?

8–9 Spot the Difference

10–11 Hidden Shapes

12–13 Web Maze

Unpack the Rucksack

6. *Compass*

10. *Carton of Fungal Jungle Juice*

15. *Binoculars*

21. *Pencil*

14–15 Flower Hopping

16–17 Crazy Maze

18–19 Rug Race

20 Giant Wordsearch

17 Bigfoot's Boot

Pig
Rat
Frog
Goat
Bear
Duck
Seal
Fish
Crow
Toucan
Seagull
Dolphin
Squirrel
Dinosaur
Elephant
Kangaroo

ANTHONY ANT'S MYSTERY MIDNIGHT FEAST

First published in Great Britain in 1998 by Orion Children's Books
a division of the Orion Publishing Group Ltd Orion House
5 Upper St Martin's Lane London WC2H 9EA

Copyright © Lorna and Graham Philpot 1998 Designed by Ian Butterworth

The right of Lorna and Graham Philpot to be identified as the author and illustrator of this work has been asserted.

A catalogue record for this book is available from The British Library

Printed and bound in Italy

ISBN 1 85881 469 3